Horses on the ranch

Saddled up and ready to ride

Sandra at age twelve

Sandra holding the reins

The Lazy B Ranch

Windmills catch the desert breezes.

# SANDRA DAY O'CONNOR

## FINDING SUSIE

ILLUSTRATED BY TOM POHRT

ALFRED A. KNOPF · NEW YORK

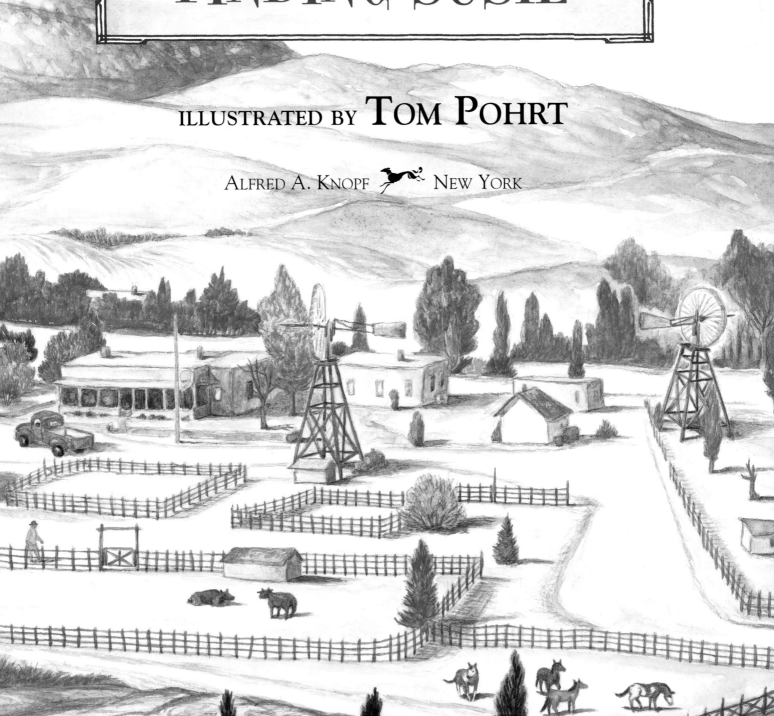

*Library of Congress Cataloging-in-Publication Data*
O'Connor, Sandra Day.
Finding Susie / by Sandra Day O'Connor ; illustrated by Tom Pohrt. — 1st ed.
p. cm.
Summary: On a ranch in the American Southwest, Sandra longs for a pet, but each time she tries to adopt a wild animal, she concludes that it will be better off where it belongs.
ISBN 978-0-375-84103-3 (trade) — ISBN 978-0-375-94103-0 (lib. bdg.)
[1. Wild animals as pets—Fiction. 2. Pets—Fiction. 3. Ranch life—Southwest, New—Fiction.
4. Southwest, New—Fiction.] I. Pohrt, Tom, ill. II. Title.
PZ7.O2226Fin 2009
[E]—dc22
2008024525

The illustrations in this book were created using watercolor.

MANUFACTURED IN CHINA
May 2009
10 9 8 7 6 5 4 3 2 1
First Edition

*To the loving memory of my parents,*
*Ada Mae and Harry Day*
*—S.D.O.*


*For Isabel and Carmen*
*—T.P.*

Sandra's summer began on a hot day beneath the pure, deep blue desert sky. She finished rereading her favorite book, and when she looked off in the distance, heat waves sparkled like ripples on a lake. Sandra loved living on the ranch, but now that school was over she would miss having other children to play with. "I wonder if this will be the year Mother and Dad will let me have a pet," she asked the sky. "Mother always says she will not allow an animal in the house. And Dad says I can just ride my horse. But it would be so nice to have a little pet to hold, to talk to, and to take care of."

A week later, Sandra was driving in the truck with her father. "Do you see what I see?" he asked. A desert tortoise was walking slowly near the ranch road.

When Sandra got out of the truck and approached him, the tortoise pulled his head and legs inside his shell. Sandra picked him up and turned him upside down. With his head and legs tucked inside, the tortoise was about the size of a dinner plate.

"Daddy, can I take the tortoise home? Please, Daddy!"

"All right, if you promise to take good care of him," said her father.

"I will," said Sandra.

Sandra put the tortoise in the front yard at the ranch house. There was grass and a low wall and a gate so the tortoise could not get out. Sandra put out a bowl of water and some lettuce and other raw vegetables. The tortoise looked strong in his hard shell, so she named him Hercules.

Hercules stayed in the yard for several weeks, eating the food Sandra put out and walking slowly around the grassy area. Sandra picked Hercules up and tried to talk to him, but he always pulled his head and legs into his shell.

Sandra brought Hercules into the kitchen a number of times. He learned to follow her to the refrigerator, where the lettuce and other vegetables were kept, in hopes of receiving more food. But Sandra was sorry that Hercules never seemed happy to see her.

"How old do you think Hercules is, Daddy?"

"Oh, it's hard to say. Desert tortoises can live up to a hundred years. In the winter, they dig deep tunnels and hibernate," said her father.

"What do you mean—'hibernate'?" said Sandra.

"They go to sleep for a few months. They don't eat, but they are able to stay alive in that condition until the weather warms and there are green leaves to eat. We used to see a lot more of them. I think they are beginning to disappear."

"It would be too bad if there were no more tortoises," said Sandra. "Do you think we should take Hercules back to the place where we found him?"

"Yes, we should probably do that before summer ends."

A few days later, her father drove Sandra and Hercules to the road where they had found him. Sandra carefully carried Hercules to a place where she could gently put him down. She put a few raw vegetables near him and said, "Be well, Hercules. Live a long time!"

Sandra knew she still wanted a pet. Later that summer, she found a very small cottontail rabbit nestled in the bushes near the windmill. The little rabbit was no bigger than her father's hand. Sandra picked her up and brought her to the house. The rabbit was trembling and afraid. Her little tail was round and white and looked like a ball of cotton. Sandra showed the rabbit to her parents and said she wanted to keep her as a pet. Her mother sighed, "I suppose you can try, but you may *not* let it loose in the house!"

Sandra named the rabbit Daisy. Her father helped her build a wire cage with a small gate she could use to reach inside and pick up the rabbit. She fed Daisy lettuce, broccoli, celery leaves, spinach, carrots, and some milk and water. The little rabbit ate most of the things Sandra gave her and grew a little larger. But Daisy did not like to be petted or held. She always seemed afraid. After a few weeks, Sandra's father said, "Wild rabbits usually prefer to live outside with other rabbits. Why don't you let Daisy go back where she came from so she can be with the other rabbits?"

"Please, Daddy. Daisy might be happier in a few more weeks. Let's keep her a little while longer," Sandra said.

But finally, Sandra decided her father was right. She went to the cage and picked up Daisy and held her. "Daisy, be good. I'm going to take you home to be with your rabbit family. I will miss you, though." Then Sandra carried Daisy back to the bushes near the windmill and put her down. Daisy hopped away without even a backward look.

On a scorching hot day, Claude, one of the cowboys, told Sandra and her father that he had seen a young coyote caught in a trap in the pasture a couple of miles away. Sandra and her father drove to the area Claude had described to try to find the coyote. There on a hill near some sagebrush, they saw the small coyote struggling to free himself from the metal trap. One of his legs was badly hurt where the trap had closed on it. Sandra's father wrapped the coyote in an empty feed sack to hold him quiet long enough to release the trap. Then he held the coyote tightly as he carefully drove back to the ranch house. "I don't know who set that trap!" Sandra's father exclaimed. "No one is allowed to trap coyotes on *this* property."

"Can we keep him, Daddy? I will take care of him and help him get well," said Sandra.

"We'll see," said her father. "Coyotes are very smart, and I know he looks a bit like a young pup, but they never get used to living with people like a dog does. I think you'll find it difficult to keep him."

"Oh, please. Let me try," she said.

"Okay. You can try, at least until his leg is better," said her dad.

When they got home, Sandra put some ointment on the coyote's injured leg and placed him in the cage she had used for Daisy. She gave him bowls of milk and water, along with some

berries and fresh hamburger meat. Sandra had read that coyotes eat many things, not just meat.

The little coyote was very restless and continuously paced in his cage. He did not want to be touched or petted. Sandra named the coyote Slim Pickins.

Claude looked at Slim and said, "Sandra, don't you know that coyotes aren't good for nothin' but killin' rabbits and baby cows and making noise at night?"

Still, Sandra tried hard to get Slim to sit down and to let her pet him. But although his leg healed, he did not want to be near a human being.

Sandra had often heard coyotes howling in the night. She knew that one coyote could sound like two or three with its different voices. But Slim never howled while he was in the cage.

Finally, Sandra told her father that she thought Slim would be better off if he could return to the desert. When they let him out near where they'd first found him, Slim ran quietly away, never once looking back. Sandra felt very sad that the coyote did not want to be her friend.

A few days later, Sandra's father was out riding his horse on a high and rough part of the ranch. He found a baby bobcat, mewing and looking hungry and lost. He looked around and could not find the mother. Finally, he picked up the bobcat kitten and put him in his jacket pocket. Back at the ranch house that evening, Sandra watched him pull the baby bobcat out of his pocket. Sandra's father got some milk and warmed it in a pan on the stove. Then he let Sandra hold the kitten and feed him, using an eyedropper to put the milk in his mouth. The kitten was very hungry and took almost a half cup of the milk. Sandra helped find a cardboard box for him and made a bed in it out of old rags.

"I thought this little cat would die if I did not take him home," said her father. "And I thought you might like to see him."

"I'm so glad," said Sandra. "I'll help take care of him." And she did. She fed him with the eyedropper. She held the little bobcat and rubbed his fur. She named the kitten Bob.

In a few months, Bob grew bigger and stronger. She took him to the bunkhouse to show to Claude. "Sandra, what are you doing with that bobcat? He'll just get big and try to eat you," he said. "Them things is mean!"

"Oh, no, Claude, I'll teach Bob to be nice. You'll see," said Sandra. And she did. Bob was friendly. He loved to be fed, petted, and scratched by Sandra. She got a ball of yarn and Bob chased it and played with it. Bob even purred like an ordinary house cat when he was happy.

But soon Bob did not look like an ordinary house cat. He was much larger, with rough fur, sharp-pointed ears, and a very short stub of a tail. One day, Sandra asked her mother for some fresh meat to feed Bob. She cut it in little pieces and put it in a dish for him. Bob sniffed and circled it. Then he arched his back and growled. When Sandra picked up a piece of the meat and held it out to Bob, he scratched her hand with his claws as he grabbed the meat. "Ouch!" she cried. "You hurt me, Bob!" Meat soon became Bob's favorite food. But Sandra never again tried to get close to him when fresh meat was around.

After two years, Bob was fully grown—about the size of a
cocker spaniel. Then one night, he just disappeared. Sandra looked
everywhere for Bob—down by the water tank, at the windmill, and
around the barn. She called his name.

"Daddy, can we get our horses and go look for Bob?" Sandra asked.

Her dad shook his head. "I don't think we should find Bob, Sandra.
He probably found another bobcat and went off to make his home
away from people. Bob will be happier out on a mountain somewhere
than with us. Maybe he will even have a family of his own."

"Well, I just miss him so much," said Sandra. "He was my friend. He kept me company and I liked him. I know he growled and scratched. But that was only once. I just hope he comes back."

The following week, Sandra and her parents drove to town to buy groceries and pick up their mail at the post office. Mr. White, the owner of the grocery store, was standing behind the counter. "Howdy, Sandra," he said. "How are you? Say, I have something to show you."

He walked outside to his house, which was behind
the store. There in the little garden by his house was
a small white dog with a curly tail. "Hello, Susie,"
said Mr. White. "I brought someone to see you."

Sandra knelt down, and Susie came up and sniffed
her and wagged her tail. Sandra gently touched
Susie's back.

"If you want to take Susie home," Mr. White said, "it will be all right. She just showed up here a few days ago, and we don't know who owns her. No one has claimed her."

"I'll ask my parents," said Sandra.

But Sandra's parents were not so sure.

"I don't know, Sandra. You haven't had much luck with your pets so far," said her mother.

Sandra's father said, "Let's see if Susie likes your company."

Susie *did* like Sandra's company.
And Sandra loved hers. Together they
explored the barns and the corrals.
They went to see Claude and the
bunkhouse. Susie even went to the
door of the house and barked as if to
say, "I'm here. Let me in!"

Sandra fed Susie and made a bed for her on the back porch.
The little dog followed Sandra wherever she went. Susie was
also friendly with Sandra's parents and all the cowboys. In fact,
sometimes Susie *smiled*. After she smiled at Sandra's mother, she
was even allowed to come inside the house.

"You know," Sandra said, "I think a dog is about the best pet I could have. Susie, I love you!" Susie just wagged her tail and smiled right back at her best friend.

Bob the bobcat

Water mills at the family ranch

Susie with Sandra's relatives and other dogs

Sandra and Chico

Sandra and her pet javelina

P9-DYE-971

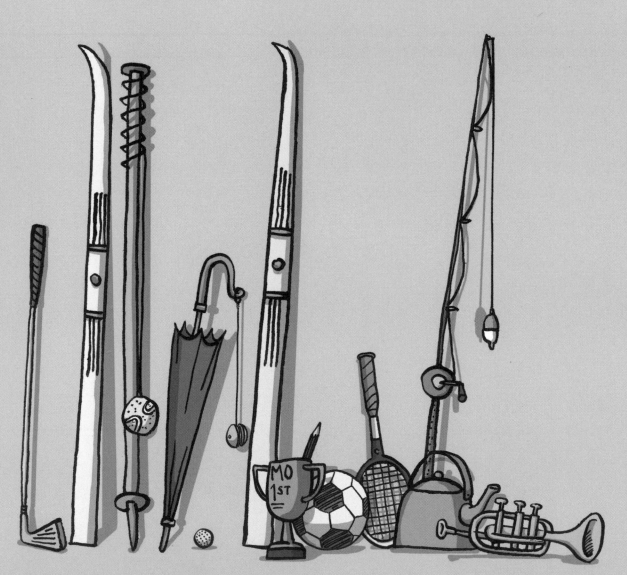

For Nicola

This edition first published in 2015 by Gecko Press
PO Box 9335, Marion Square, Wellington 6141, New Zealand
info@geckopress.com

Distributed in New Zealand by Upstart Distribution, www.upstartpress.co.nz
Distributed in Australia by Scholastic Australia, www.scholastic.com.au
Distributed in the United Kingdom by Bounce Sales & Marketing,
www.bouncemarketing.co.uk
Distributed in the United States and Canada by Lerner Publishing Group,
www.lernerbooks.com

First American edition published in 2015 by Gecko Press USA,
an imprint of Gecko Press Ltd.
A catalog record for this book is available from the US Library of Congress.

A catalogue record for this book is available from the National Library of New Zealand.

**creative nz**
ARTS COUNCIL OF NEW ZEALAND TOI AOTEAROA

Gecko Press acknowledges the generous support of Creative New Zealand.
Designed and art directed by Vida & Luke Kelly, New Zealand
Printed in China by Everbest Printing Co Ltd, an accredited ISO 14001
& FSC certified printer

ISBN hardback: 978-1-927271-98-8
ISBN paperback: 978-1-927271-99-5
E-book available

# HELLO WORLD!

Paul Beavis

GECKO PRESS

# Mr. and Mrs. Mo were busy.

They had no time to play.

"It's not fair," said the monster.

"What about me?"

"I'm sorry," said Mrs. Mo.

"We'll do something fun tomorrow."

Then he had an idea.

"I'm packing my bag,"
said the monster.
"I'm off to see the world."

"How exciting,"
said Mrs. Mo.
"Can I make you
a sandwich?"

"I'm okay," said the monster.

"I've got everything I need."

Soon home was far behind.

"Now this is what I call fun,"

said the monster.

A little later the monster saw a hill.

"I could climb to the top of that hill," said the monster.
"It's not far. It's just around the corner."

**"Whoopee!"** yelled the monster.

"Poor Mrs. Mo, missing all this fun."

And on he marched.

But after every corner, the monster found another corner.

"How much further?"
he grumbled.

"Oh dear,"
said the monster.

"I wish I'd stayed at home,"
said the monster.
"I wish I'd waited till tomorrow."

"Mrs. Mo!"
said the monster.
"You found me."

"I thought you might
be missing a few things,"
said Mrs. Mo.

"Do you have time for a sandwich?"
asked Mrs. Mo.

"Maybe just the one,"
said the monster.

Soon he felt much better.

"Come on, Mrs. Mo," he said.

"We've got a hill to climb!"

And together Mrs. Mo and the monster
began to climb.

"Don't worry," said the monster.
"We're nearly there."

"Hello, world!"
said the monster.
"And hello, Mr. Mo!"

"Shall we go home now?" asked Mrs. Mo.

"I can show you the way!" said the monster.

"That was fun," said Mrs. Mo.

"You're welcome,"
said the monster.
"Now, what shall
we do tomorrow?"